牡蛎男孩：我生来一半是男孩，一半是海鲜。我的爸爸和妈妈，一心只想拿我换一个新的妹妹。

锚儿：我的妈妈，爱上我的爸爸。生下我之后，爸爸离家，我的妈妈在海底望得眼巴巴。

枯枝男孩：我爱上了火柴女郎。你应该不难想象，那真的跟飞蛾扑火没什么两样。

污渍小子：只要不消十分钟，穿在我身上的新衣，就全变得脏兮兮。

詹姆士：跟众人相比，我实在不怪异。我只是，刚被一只大灰熊攻击而已。

蒂姆·波顿的怪诞世界

THE MELANCHOLY DEATH OF OYSTER BOY AND OTHER STORIES

牡蛎男孩忧郁之死

鬼才导演蒂姆·波顿唯一悲惨故事集

[美] 蒂 姆 · 波 顿 / 著　　林 则 良 / 译

天津出版传媒集团

天津人民出版社

图书在版编目（CIP）数据

蒂姆·波顿的怪诞世界：牡蛎男孩忧郁之死：鬼才导演蒂姆·波顿唯一悲惨故事集/（美）蒂姆·波顿著；林则良译. --天津：天津人民出版社，2018.3

书名原文：THE MELANCHOLY DEATH OF OYSTER BOY AND OTHER STORIES

ISBN 978-7-201-12852-8

Ⅰ.①蒂… Ⅱ.①蒂… ②林… Ⅲ.①故事－作品集－美国－现代 Ⅳ.①I712.45

中国版本图书馆CIP数据核字（2017）第329506号

著作权合同登记号 02-2017-292

蒂姆·波顿的怪诞世界：牡蛎男孩忧郁之死

DIMU · BODUN DE GUAIDAN SHIJIE: MULI NANHAI YOUYU ZHISI

出　　版　天津人民出版社
出 版 人　黄　沛
地　　址　天津市和平区西康路35号康岳大厦
邮政编码　300051
邮购电话　（022）23332469
网　　址　http://www.tjrmcbs.com
电子邮箱　tjrmcbs@126.com

责任编辑　王昊静
策划编辑　刘丽娜
装帧设计　lemon

制版印刷　北京市十月印刷有限公司
经　　销　新华书店
开　　本　889×1194毫米　1/32
印　　张　4.75
字　　数　20千字
版次印次　2018年3月第1版　2018年3月第1次印刷
定　　价　39.80元

献给丽莎·玛莉

For Lisa Marie

目录 | Contents |

热恋中的枯枝男孩和火柴女郎

枯枝男孩喜欢火柴女郎，
他对她十分中意，
他喜欢她俏丽身影，
他觉得她火辣热情。

Stick Boy and Match Girl in Love

Stick Boy liked Match Girl.
He liked her a lot.
He liked her cute figure.
He thought she was hot.

不过爱火可曾
为枯枝和火柴燃起？
当然那爱火一发不可收拾，
他转眼烧个不停。

But could a flame ever burn
for a match and a stick?
It did quite literally;
he burned up pretty quick.

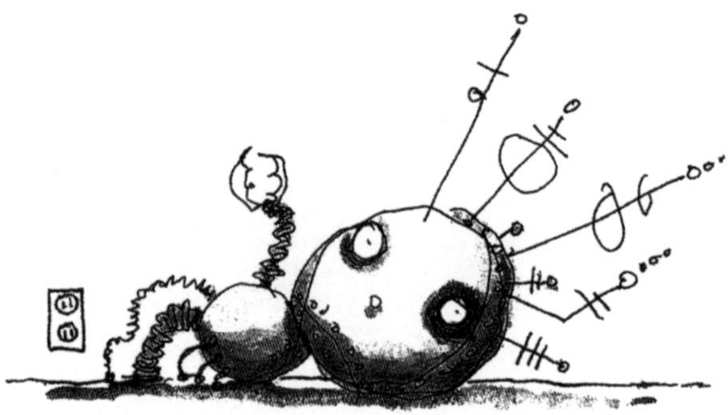

机器人男孩

史密斯太太和史密斯先生美满幸福，
他们是很平凡很快乐的妻子和丈夫。
一天他们得知了一个好消息，
这消息让史密斯先生欢天喜地。
史密斯太太要当妈了，
所以他就要做爸了！
然而他们的喜悦结晶却出了点儿岔，
它怎么看怎么不像个人，
它是个机器娃儿！

Robot Boy

Mr. and Mrs. Smith had a wonderful life.
They were a normal, happy husband and wife.
One day they got news that made Mr. Smith glad.
Mrs. Smith would be a mom,
which would make him the dad!
But something was wrong with their bundle of joy.
It wasn’t human at all.
It was a robot boy!

他既没温度也不惹人疼，
他甚至没肤又没皮，
除了冷冰冰、薄怯怯的一层锡，
还有那头上伸出的管子和电线。
他躺在那儿目不转睛，
非死亦非生。

唯有接上延长线、
插入墙上的电插头，
那一刻他才显得灵气活现。

He wasn't warm and cuddly
and he didn't have skin.
Instead, there was a cold, thin layer of tin.
There were wires and tubes sticking out of his head.
He just lay there and stared,
not living or dead.

The only time he seemed alive at all
was with a long extension cord
plugged into the wall.

史密斯先生对着医生吼吼叫叫：
“你到底对我儿子动了什么手脚？
他没血也没肉，
是个铝合金怪兽！”

Mr. Smith yelled at the doctor,
“What have you done to my boy?
He’s not flesh and blood.
He’s aluminum alloy!”

医生回以轻声细语：
“我接下来要告诉你的事，
听起来实在难以置信。
不过你并非是
这怪小孩的亲生父亲。
你看，连小孩到底是男是女，
到现在依旧扑朔迷离，
不过我们认为孩子的亲生父亲，
是一只微波搅拌机。”

The doctor said gently,
“What I’m going to say
will sound pretty wild.
But you’re not the father
of this strange-looking child.
You see, there is still some question
about the child’s gender,
but we think that its father
is a microwave blender.”

从此史密斯家的生活，
雪上加霜且鸡犬不宁。
史密斯太太恨她老公，
他则恨他老婆。
他永远无法原谅，
老婆背着他暗地私通，
而对象竟然会是——
厨房的一台电器。

如今机器人男孩，
已长成一位年轻男子。
虽然他老被人错认为——
是一只垃圾箱。

The Smiths' lives were now filled
with misery and strife.
Mrs. Smith hated her husband,
and he hated his wife.
He never forgave her unholy alliance:
a sexual encounter
with a kitchen appliance.

And Robot Boy
grew to be a young man.
Though he was often mistaken
for a garbage can.

瞪大眼女孩

我认识那么一个女孩，
光站在那里瞪大双眼。
不管看东还是看西，
她一点儿都不在意。

Staring Girl

I once knew a girl
who would just stand there and stare.
At anyone or anything,
she seemed not to care.

她会对地面瞪大眼。

She'd stare at the ground.

她会对天空瞪大眼。

She’d stare at the sky.

她会瞪你瞪好几个小时，
而你还是一头雾水。

She'd stare at you for hours,
and you'd never know why.

1st
2
3
1
2
3

不过自从她荣获本地的瞪眼冠军，

But after winning the local staring contest,

她那双大眼最后终于
赢得最妥善的休息。

She finally gave her eyes
a well-deserved rest.

眼中钉男孩

双眼钉了铁钉的男孩，
在摆设他那棵铝树。
树的模样看来真滑稽，
那全是他雾里看花的缘故。

The Boy with Nails in His Eyes

The Boy with Nails in His Eyes
put up his aluminum tree.
It looked pretty strange
because he couldn't really see.

脸上都是眼睛的女孩

那天在公园，
我非常非常吃惊；
我遇到一个女孩，
脸上都是眼睛。

The Girl with Many Eyes

One day in the park
I had quite a surprise.
I met a girl
who had many eyes.

她人长得真是漂亮，
（而且还真吓人一跳！）
我注意到她有张樱桃小嘴，
所以我们开始东聊西聊。

我们谈及鲜花朵朵，
我们聊她课堂念的诗，
我们还聊到若她得戴眼镜，
那可真会麻烦多多。

She was really quite pretty
(and also quite shocking!)
and I noticed she had a mouth,
so we ended up talking.

We talked about flowers,
and her poetry classes,
and the problems she'd have
if she ever wore glasses.

能遇见一个女孩
满脸都是眼睛，
这实在叫人开心。
不过要是她落泪伤心，
你就会变成一只落汤鸡。

It's great to know a girl
who has so many eyes,
but you really get wet
when she breaks down and cries.

污渍小子传奇

所有的超级英雄里，
就数他最怪异，
他不开时髦跑车，
也没半点儿超自然力。

若和超人蝙蝠侠相比，
我想他算安分守己，
不过我觉得他真神奇，
污渍小子就是他的英名。

Stain Boy

Of all the super heroes,
the strangest one by far,
doesn't have a special power,
or drive a fancy car.

Next to Superman and Batman,
I guess he must seem tame.
But to me he is quite special,
and Stain Boy is his name.

5

他没办法绕着高楼大厦飞，
也没办法跑得比高速火车快；
但说到留下脏兮兮的污渍，
这家伙可是盖世天才。

He can’t fly around tall buildings,
or outrun a speeding train,
the only talent he seems to have
is to leave a nasty stain.

我知道他有时也伤透脑筋，
既不会飞，不会游，也不会跑，
况且正因他唯一的超能力，
他送干洗的账单堆得比天还高。

Sometimes I know it bothers him,
that he can’t run or swim or fly,
and because of this one ability,
his dry cleaning bill’s sky-high.

牡蛎男孩忧郁之死

The Melancholy Death of Oyster Boy

他在沙丘上求婚。

He proposed in the dunes.

他们在海边成亲。

They were wed by the sea.

在卡普利岛，他们庆祝
为期九天的蜜月旅行。

Their nine-day-long honeymoon
was on the isle of Capri.

晚餐他们点了一客特大号、
一锅全是淡菜和鱼的炖汤。
当他品尝那锅海鲜，
做新娘的她默默许下心愿。

For their supper they had one spectacular dish—
a simmering stew of mollusks and fish.
And while he savored the broth,
her bride's heart made a wish.

心愿成真——她生下一个小娃。
不过这小家伙可有半点儿人样?
好吧,
约莫七七八八。

十只手指十只脚趾,
他会消化,会看东西。
他会听,他有感应。
但一切正常?
说来未必。
这非自然的生命,这祸害,这病源,
是他们一切苦难的起始与终结。

That wish did come true—she gave birth to a baby.
But was this little one human?
Well,
maybe.

Ten fingers, ten toes,
he had plumbing and sight.
He could hear, he could feel,
but normal?
Not quite.
This unnatural birth, this canker, this blight,
was the start and the end and the sum of their plight.

她对着大夫埋怨：
“他不可能是我亲生骨肉。
他浑身都是海洋、水草和盐水的味道。”

She railed at the doctor,
“He cannot be mine.
He smells of the ocean, of seaweed and brine.”

“你应该感到庆幸，不过就在上个星期，
我还治疗过一个女孩，有着三只耳朵和一张鸟喙。
你儿子生来有一半是牡蛎，
这不能归罪于我。
……
倒要问问你有没有闪过这样的念头，
不如举家搬迁到海滩上头？”

“You should count yourself lucky, for only last week,
I treated a girl with three ears and a beak.
That your son is half oyster
you cannot blame me.
...have you considered, by chance,
a small home by the sea?”

不知该如何取名，
他们随口叫他山姆，
或者，偶尔也叫他——
“那个看起来像蛤蜊的东西。”
每个人都在揣测但无人知晓，
小山姆何时会脱壳而出？

Not knowing what to name him,
they just called him Sam,
or, sometimes,
“that thing that looks like a clam.”

Everyone wondered, but no one could tell,
When would young Oyster Boy come out of his shell?

一天汤普生家的四胞胎在外偷看，
他们喊他“蚵仔”，然后一哄而散。

When the Thompson quadruplets espied him one day,
they called him a bivalve and ran quickly away.

某个春日午后，
山姆被遗弃在滂沱雨中，
在海景街和主街交口的西南角落，
他凝望着雨水打转
然后看它们一路流进排水沟。

One spring afternoon,
Sam was left in the rain.
At the southwestern corner of Seaview and Main,
he watched the rain water as it swirled
down the drain.

他母亲人在高速公路
交通瘫痪的线道上头，
她猛拍汽车仪表板——
她无法承受
不断在心头翻腾的悲恸、
沮丧和苦痛。

His mom on the freeway
in the breakdown lane
was pounding the dashboard—
she couldn't contain
the ever-rising grief,
frustration,
and pain.

“说真的，甜心，”她说，
“我可不是在说笑，
但我一直闻到鱼腥味，
我想那来自咱们的宝贝。
我不想说，但我必须说，
你不能把自己的问题，全推给咱们生的那小家伙。”

他敷软膏，他涂药膏，
结果全身红肿。
他尝试各种方法
还试图吃酊剂来力图振作。
结果他又痛又痒又抽搐又流血。

“Really, sweetheart,” she said,
“I don’t mean to make fun,
but something smells fishy
and I think it’s our son.
I don’t like to say this, but it must be said,
you’re blaming our son for your problems in bed.”

He tried salves, he tried ointments
that turned everything red.
He tried potions and lotions
and tincture of lead.
He ached and he itched and he twitched and he bled.

根据大夫诊断：
“我不敢百分百确定，
但问题之所在可能就是解药之所在。
据说牡蛎可以增进雄风，
也许把你儿子吃下肚里，
能让你忙活好一阵。”

The doctor diagnosed,
“I can’t be quite sure,
but the cause of the problem may also be the cure.
They say oysters improve your sexual powers.
Perhaps eating your son
would help you do it for hours!”

他蹑手蹑脚，
他偷偷走近，
他额头冒着汗，
他嘴唇——在说谎。
“儿子呀，你快乐吗？我不是有意打探，
不过你是否向往天国？
你是否想过一死百了？”

He came on tiptoe,
he came on the sly,
sweat on his forehead,
and on his lips—a lie.
“Son, are you happy? I don’t mean to pry,
but do you dream of Heaven?
Have you wanted to die?”

山姆眨了两次眼，
不说一句话。
老爸握了握菜刀，而后松了松领带。

Sam blinked his eyes twice.
but made no reply.
Dad fingered his knife and loosened his tie.

当他举起自己的儿子，
山姆滴了汁在他大衣上头。
他把壳靠在唇上，
山姆便沿着他的喉咙滑落。

As he picked up his son,
Sam dripped on his coat.
With the shell to his lips,
Sam slipped down his throat.

他们在海边的沙地草草埋了他
——念一段祷词，滴一滴眼泪——
下午三点就回到了家。

牡蛎男孩墓上插着灰白的浮木十字架。
他的墓志铭写在沙上，
允诺他重回天父的怀抱。

They buried him quickly in the sand by the sea
—sighed a prayer, wept a tear—
and were back home by three.

A cross of gray driftwood marked Oyster Boy's grave.
Words write in the sand
promised Jesus would save.

不过一阵涨潮，就使他一生的记忆随波飘逝。

But his memory was lost with one high-tide wave.

回到家安心躺卧在床，
他亲吻她，然后说：
“我们来吧。”

Back home safe in bed,
he kissed her and said,
“Let’s give it a whirl.”

“但这一次，” 她轻声细语，
“愿我们生的是个女娃。”

“But this time, ” she whispered, “we’ll wish for a girl. ”

巫毒女郎

她的肌肤是一袭白布，
她的全身缝缝补补，
还有一堆彩色大头针，
从她的心脏里头刺出。

她有一只漂亮、
不断环绕旋转的电眼，
一只能够妖惑催眠、
众家鲁男子的媚眼。

Voodoo Girl

Her skin is white cloth,
and she's all sewn apart
and she has many colored pins
sticking out of her heart.

She has a beautiful set
of hypno-disk eyes,
the ones that she uses
to hypnotize guys.

各式各样的僵尸，
对她深深着魔。
她甚至网罗了僵尸一只，
远道来自法国。

She has many different zombies
who are deeply in her trance.
She even has a zombie
who was originally from France.

不过她知道自己深受诅咒，
这躲也躲不掉的厄运。
一旦哪个人
想接近她，
那些彩色大头针就会愈刺愈深。

But she knows she has a curse on her,
a curse she cannot win.
For if someone gets
too close to her,
the pins stick farther in.

S

污渍小子别开生面的圣诞节

圣诞佳节，污渍小子收到一件新制服，
洁白干爽，烫得整整齐齐，
暖和又舒服。

Stain Boy's Special Christmas

For Christmas, Stain Boy got a new uniform.
It was clean and well pressed,
comfy and warm.

但不消几分钟，
（绝不超过十分钟）

But in a few short minutes,
(no longer than ten)

湿漉漉、油腻腻的污渍，
又全身皆是。

those wet, greasy stains
started forming again.

化作一张眠床的
女孩

自从那一天，
她摘下某种稀奇的猫柳，
她的头颅就开始鼓胀发白，
轻柔，一如枕头。

她的肌肤，已转变，
层层叠叠，且质变，
现在已改头换面，
呈百分百纯棉。

The Girl
Who Turned into a Bed

It happened that day
she picked some strange pussy willow.
Her head swelled up white
and soft as a pillow.

Her skin, which had turned
all flaky and rotten,
was now replaced
with 100% cotton.

而她身上的器官和躯干，
已生成羽翼的模样，
长成漂亮的摆设，
由床垫和弹簧构成。

Through her organs and torso
she sprouted like wings,
a beautiful set
of mattress and springs.

这实在怪异得叫人胆战心惊，
我为此开始啜泣。
不过哭过之后，
至少我有个好去处，
能一觉到天明。

It was so terribly strange
that I started to weep.
But at least after that
I had a nice place to sleep.

罗伊，那个剧毒男孩

我们这群认识他的人
——他的亲朋——
都管他叫罗伊。
对其他不认识他的人，
他则是“那个可怕的剧毒男孩”。

Roy, the Toxic Boy

To those of us who knew him
—his friends—
we called him Roy.
To others he was known
as that horrible Toxic Boy.

hair
spray

他热爱阿摩尼亚和石棉，
他还酷爱大量二手烟。
他所赖以维生的空气，
会让大多数人缺氧窒息！

他最爱的小玩具，
是一小罐喷雾器；
他可以一整天不吵不闹坐在那里，
三不五时就摇摇喷喷那罐喷雾器。

He loved ammonia and asbestos,
and lots of cigarette smoke.

What he breathed in for air
would make most people choke!

His very favorite toy
was a can of aerosol spray;
he'd sit quietly and shake it,
and spray it all the day.

在天寒地冻的清晨，
他会站在车库里，
静待车子起火发动，
好让自己沉浸在引擎废气之中。

He'd stand inside of the garage
in the early-morning frost,
waiting for the car to start
and fill him with exhaust.

绝无仅有独此一回，
我亲眼看见剧毒男孩泪眼汪汪。
只因当时有食盐少许，
恰巧落入他的眼眶。

The one and only time
I ever saw Toxic Boy cry
when some sodium chloride
got into his eye.

有天为了呼吸新鲜空气，
他们把他安置在花园里。

他的脸色顿时惨白，
他的身体开始僵硬。

One day for fresh air
they put him in the garden.

His face went deathly pale
and his body began to harden.

在他短暂一生的弥留之际，
他病态蔫蔫，绝望至极。
谁会想到呼吸户外空气，
竟会置人于绝境死地？

The final gasp of his short life
was sickly with despair.
Whoever thought that you could die
from breathing outdoor air?

当罗伊的灵魂脱离身躯，
我们全体为他默哀致敬。
他的灵魂直上天际，
徒留破洞在臭氧层里。

As Roy's soul left his body,
we all said a silent prayer.
It drifted up to heaven
and left a hole in the ozone layer.

詹姆斯

真不高明，圣诞老公公给了詹姆斯一只泰迪熊当礼物，万万没想到他早些时候，才被一只大灰熊撕扯得体无完肤。

James

Unwisely, Santa offered a teddy bear to James, unaware that he had been mauled by a grizzly earlier that year.

枯枝男孩的
圣诞季节

枯枝男孩发现他的圣诞树怎么看
都比他健壮。

Stick Boy's Festive Season

Stick Boy noticed that his Christmas tree looked healthier than he did.

布利起司小子

布利起司小子有两次梦见，
他浑圆的大头只剩一小片。

Brie Boy

Brie Boy had a dream he only had twice,
that his full, round head was only a slice.

其他小孩都不肯和布利起司小子一起玩……
……但他至少和优质夏多内[1]是天生绝配。

The other children never let Brie Boy play…
…but at least he went well with a nice Chardonnay.

| Note |

1 夏多内，葡萄品种，可用来酿制白酒。

木乃伊男孩

他没有软香粉嫩的肌肤，
也没有圆滚滚的小肥肚；
他里面空空外壳坚硬，
他是个小男孩木乃伊。

“医生，拜托行行好，
告诉我们到底是谁造的孽？
为何我们的一场欢快，
却换来这破布一团？”

Mummy Boy

He wasn’t soft and pink
with a fat little tummy;
he was hard and hollow,
a little boy mummy.

“Tell us, please, doctor,
the reason or cause,
why our bundle of joy
is just a bundle of gauze.”

“我的诊断是，”他说，
“姑且不论是好是坏，
你们的儿子是遭到了
古法老王诅咒的贻害。”

“My diagnosis,” he said,
“for better or worse,
is that your son is the result
of an old pharaoh’s curse.”

当天晚上他们谈了又谈，
他们儿子离奇古怪的处境。
他们管他叫：“一件
被考古探险队遗弃的次级品。”

他们紧抓脑袋寻思，
那些复杂的科学解释，
但最终假设那只不过是，
超自然的投胎转世。

That night they talked
of their son's odd condition—
they called him "a reject
from an archaeological expedition."

They thought of some complex
scientific explanation,
but assumed it was simple
supernatural reincarnation.

和其他的幼龄小娃娃，
他只一起玩过两次
古代献祭的游戏。
（不过娃娃们全都吓跑，嚷着：
“你真不是个好东西！”）

With the other young tots
he only played twice,
an ancient game of virgin sacrifice.
(But the kids ran away, saying, “You aren’t very nice.”)

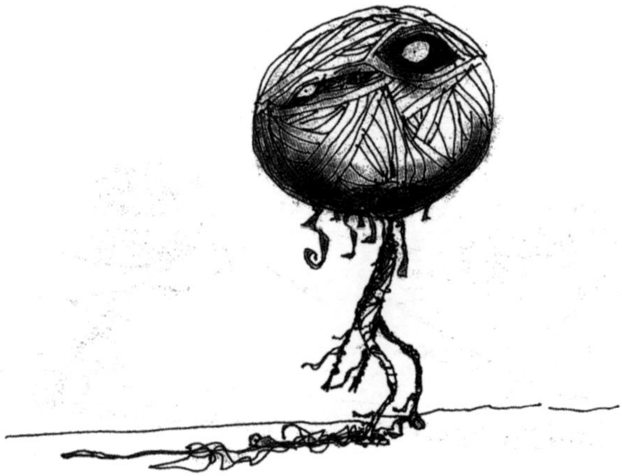

孤独一人饱受嫌弃，木乃伊男孩暗自落泪，
然后他走向储藏柜，
那里摆着好吃的零食。

Alone and rejected, Mummy Boy wept,
then went to the cabinet
where the snack food was kept.

Kellogg's
SUGAR FROSTED
TANNA
LEAVES

他用木乃伊尸布的衣袖拭去泪湿的眼窝，
倒了一碗沾满糖霜的唐纳叶[1]入座。

He wiped his wet sockets with his mummified sleeves,
and sat down to a bowl of sugar-frosted tanna leaves.

| Note |

1 唐纳叶，不存在的虚构植物名，
常出现在木乃伊电影或小说当中，
有吸引并控制木乃伊的药效。

一天天色晦暗而阴森，
雾茫茫之中，
跑出一只苍白的木乃伊小狗。

One dark, gloomy day,
from out of the fog,
appeared a little white mummy dog.

为了这新捡到的绷带宠物，
他着实费了不少工夫，
他还为它盖了一间
仿照埃及金字塔的狗屋。

For his newfound wrapped pet,
he did many things,
like building a dog house
à la Pyramid of Kings.

一天时候已晚，
转眼天就要黑了。
木乃伊男孩牵着狗，
来到公园散散步。

It was late in the day—
just before dark.
Mummy Boy took his dog
for a walk in the park.

公园里冷冷清清，
触目所及只有一只松鼠，
还有一个墨西哥女孩的生日派对。

男孩女孩玩得正开心，
却留意到那个像纸浆糊出来的玩意。

The park was empty
except for a squirrel,
and a birthday party for a Mexican girl.

The boys and girls had all started to play,
but noticed that thing that looked like papier mâché.

“你看，是个皮纳塔[1]，”
其中一个男孩说：
“我们快把它敲开来，
里面会有玩具和糖果。”

他们拿了一支球棒，
朝他的大头猛击。
木乃伊男孩不支倒地，
最后终于当场毙命。

“Look, it’s a piñata,”
said one of the boys,
“let’s crack it wide open
and get the candy and toys.”

They took a baseball bat
and whacked open his head.
Mummy Boy fell to the ground;
he finally was dead.

| Note |

1 皮纳塔，是一种用纸或纸浆糊成像灯笼的东西，色彩缤纷，挂在树上或天花板，里面藏有糖果或玩具，小孩会用棍棒将之打破。此习俗源自墨西哥，常在生日、圣诞或复活节时用来庆祝。

在他的大头壳里，
既没糖果，也没奖品，
只有几只迷路的甲虫，
大大小小不一。

Inside of his head
were no candy or prizes,
just a few stray beetles
of various sizes.

垃圾女孩

从前有个女孩，
她整个人就是垃圾。
她怎么看怎么肮脏，
怎么闻怎么像臭鼬。

她总是闷闷不乐，
三不五时陷入低潮——这或许就是因为，
她花太多时间混垃圾堆。

Junk Girl

There once was a girl
who was made up of junk.
She looked really dirty,
and she smelled like a skunk.

She was always unhappy,
or in one of her slumps—perhaps 'cause she spent
so much time down in the dumps.

她唯一开朗的时刻，
全仰赖一位名叫史丹的家伙。
他就住附近，
他专捡垃圾。

The only bright moment
was from a guy named Stan.
He was the neighborhood
garbage man.

他很爱她，
而且还跟她求了亲，
只不过她早将自己，
许给了垃圾辗碎机。

He loved her a lot
and made a marriage proposal,
but she'd already thrown herself
down a garbage disposal.

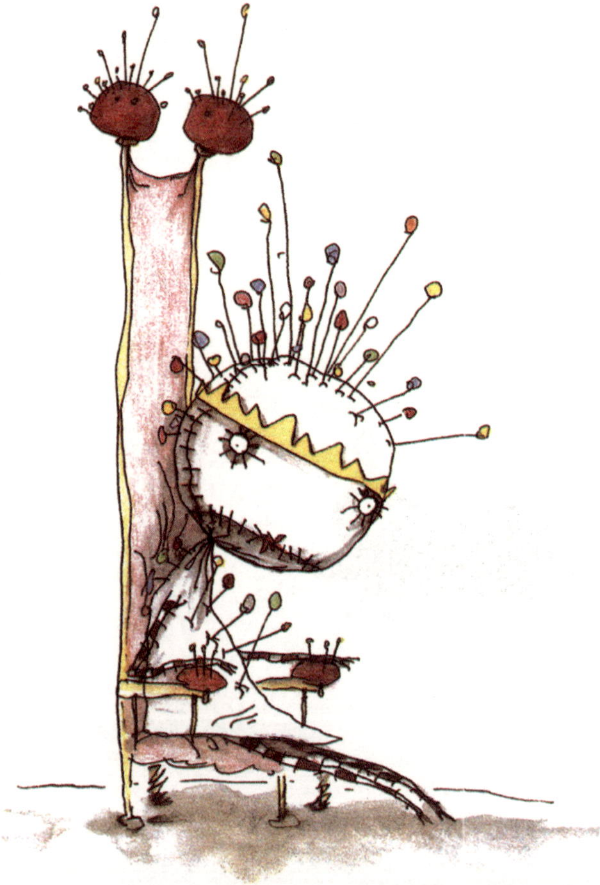

针插女王

对针插女王来说，
日子真的难过，
她一坐上王位宝座，
针就穿脾而过。

The Pin Cushion Queen

Life isn't easy
for the Pin Cushion Queen.
When she sits on her throne
pins push through her spleen.

香瓜大头

从前有个忧郁的香瓜大头，
终日坐在那边，
一心只想早日离开人间。

Melonhead

There once was a morose melonhead,
who sat there all day
and wished he were dead.

不过你得当心，
不要随便许愿。
因为他听见的最后一声，
是震耳欲聋的踩碎瓜声。

But you should be careful
about the things that you wish.
Because the last thing he heard
was a deafening squish.

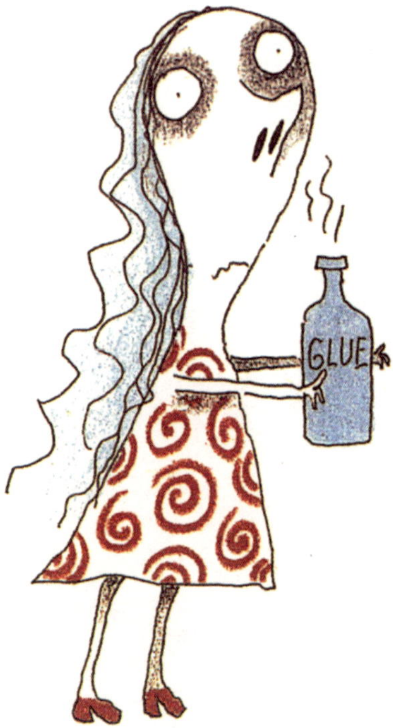
GLUE

苏

为了避免法律诉讼，
我们姑且叫她苏，
（不然就叫“那个女孩爱把胶
吸得稀里呼噜”）。

Sue

To avoid a lawsuit,
we'll just call her Sue
(or "that girl who likes
to sniff lots of glue").

我之所以敢断言
她有这般恶习，
全在她一擤鼻涕，

The reason I know
that this is the case
is when she blows her nose,

舒洁[1]就黏上脸去。

kleenex sticks to her face.

| Note |

1 舒洁，全球最知名的面巾纸品牌之一。

吉米，那个丑不拉叽的企鹅男孩

“我叫吉米，
不过我朋友都只叫我：
‘那个丑不拉叽的企鹅男孩。’”

Jimmy, the Hideous Penguin Boy

“My name is Jimmy,
but my friends just call me
‘the hideous penguin boy.’”

焦炭男孩

圣诞佳节，
焦炭男孩一如往常收到一小块煤当礼物，
这让他非常开心。

Char Boy

For Christmas,
Char Boy received his usual lump of coal,
which made him very happy.

圣诞佳节，
焦炭男孩收到一件小玩意儿，
不是往常的一小块煤，
这让他百思不得其解。

For Christmas,
Char Boy received a small present instead of
his usual lump of coal,
which confused him very much.

圣诞佳节，
焦炭男孩被误以为是一堆脏兮兮的煤灰，
被一把扫到大街上去。

For Christmas,
Char Boy was mistaken for a dirty fireplace
and swept out into the street.

锚儿

曾经有那么一个女孩，
她来自蔚蓝大海。
而只有那么一个地方，
她一心深深向往。

为了一个名叫沃克的男子，
那个在乐团里弹唱的男子。
她离开大海，
投奔陆地异乡。

Anchor Baby

There was a beautiful girl
who came from the sea.
And there was just one place
that she wanted to be.

With a man named Walker
who played in a band.
She would leave the ocean
and come onto the land.

他是她唯一、
她唯一的心之所欲。
她费尽一切心机，
欲虏获他神出鬼没的魅影。

然而他们的生命境遇，
却始终毫无交集。
她在陆上千回百折，
独自一人四处碰壁。

He was the one
that she wanted the most.
And she tried everything
to capture this ghost.

But throughout all their lives
they never connected.
She wandered the earth
alone and rejected.

她让自己看起来开心，
她让自己看起来悲戚，
她尝试占星，
性爱和巫术。

什么也无法让他们结合，
除非一样东西也许……
只是也许……
能将他们的灵魂以锚固定
——他们有了自己的小孩。

She tried looking happy
She tried looking tragic.
She tried astral projecting,
sex, and black magic.

Nothing could join them,
except maybe one thing,
just maybe...
something to anchor their spirits....
They had a baby.

但是为了生出这个孩子，
他们得动用一台起重机。
衔接婴儿的那条脐带，
看来就是铁链无疑。

它又丑又黑，
而且硬得像铁茶壶。
它没有粉嫩的肌肤，
只有沉重铅灰的金属。

But to give birth to the baby
they needed a crane.
The umbilical cord
was in the form of a chain.

It was ugly and gloomy,
and as hard as a kettle.
It had no pink skin,
just heavy gray metal.

小婴儿原本生来，
该让他俩厮守一起，
现在却让他们，
笼罩在凄风苦雨的阴霾里。

The baby that was meant
to bring them together,
just shrouded them both
in a cloud of foul weather.

于是沃克趁机开溜，
跑回乐团弹弹唱唱。
就从那一天起，
他几乎只待在陆上。

留下她只身一人，
和她铅灰的锚儿；
一切如此难过沉闷，
终究让她直往下沉。

So Walker took off
to play with the band.
And from that day on,
he stayed mainly on land.

And she was alone
with her gray baby anchor,
who got so oppressive
that it eventually sank her.

当她沉到海底深处，
她的愿望已成泡沫，
唯独她、她的锚儿……
和几只稀稀落落的鱼儿。

As she went to the bottom,
not fulfilling her wish,
it was her, and her baby...
and a few scattered fish.

trick
or
treat

牡蛎男孩出门去

迎接万圣节，
牡蛎男孩决心像其他人一样欢度佳节。

Oyster Boy Steps Out

For Halloween,
Oyster Boy decided to go as a human.

Acknowledgments

感谢

Michael McDowell, Jill Jacobs Brack,

Rodney Kizziah, Eva Quiroz

以及

David Szanto